Dear Parent:
Your child's love of reading starts here!

Every child learns to read in a different way and at his or her own speed. Some go back and forth between reading levels and read favorite books again and again. Others read through each level in order. You can help your young reader improve and become more confident by encouraging his or her own interests and abilities. From books your child reads with you to the first books he or she reads alone, there are I Can Read Books for every stage of reading:

SHARED READING
Basic language, word repetition, and whimsical illustrations, ideal for sharing with your emergent reader

BEGINNING READING
Short sentences, familiar words, and simple concepts for children eager to read on their own

READING WITH HELP
Engaging stories, longer sentences, and language play for developing readers

READING ALONE
Complex plots, challenging vocabulary, and high-interest topics for the independent reader

ADVANCED READING
Short paragraphs, chapters, and exciting themes for the perfect bridge to chapter books

I Can Read Books have introduced children to the joy of reading since 1957. Featuring award-winning authors and illustrators and a fabulous cast of beloved characters, I Can Read Books set the standard for beginning readers.

A lifetime of discovery begins with the magical words **"I Can Read!"**

Visit www.icanread.com for information on enriching your child's reading experience.

For Marley
—R.S.

 For information address HarperCollins Children's Books, a division of HarperCollins Publishers, 195 Broadway, New York, NY 10007.
www.icanread.com
Library of Congress Cataloging-in-Publication Data is available.
ISBN 978-0-06-197858-6 (trade bdg.) —ISBN 978-0-06-197857-9 (pbk.)

14 15 16 SCP 10 9 8 7 6 5 4 ❖ First Edition

Splat the Cat and the Duck with No Quack

Based on the bestselling books
by Rob Scotton

Cover art and text by Rob Scotton
Interior illustrations by Robert Eberz

HARPER
An Imprint of HarperCollins*Publishers*

splat

Splat's bike went clickity clack
as he rode along a bumpy track
to Cat School.
Suddenly, the wheel of the bike
got stuck in a crack.

With a whack and a smack,

Splat tumbled onto the track.

Splat found himself nose to beak

with a funny duck.

The funny duck had a little book.

The duck gave Splat a funny look.

"How odd!" said Splat.

This duck was strangely quiet.

"A duck lacking in quacking,"

said Splat.

"That's not right!"

“Don’t worry, Duck,” said Splat.
“You must be lost.
I’ll take you back to the pond.
I will help you
get your quack back.”

Splat picked up the duck
with the little book
and put both in his backpack.
"Take care in there," said Splat.
"And don't sit on
my fish-stick snack."

Splat put his backpack back on,
got on his bike,
and set off again
along the bumpy track
toward the pond.

Splat's bike
went clickity clickity clack
clack clack.

Splat stopped by the pond
and opened his backpack.
Duck popped out,
looked about,
then popped back in again.

"Maybe Duck isn't lost," Splat said.
"Mrs. Wimpydimple
will know what to do."
And Splat wobbled his way
back on the track to Cat School.

When Splat got to school,
he parked his bike
in the bike-rack shack
and dropped his backpack
on the bumpy track.

Duck looked out from a crack
in Splat's backpack.
Duck saw Spike's silly grin
and had a panic attack.

Duck jumped out
of Splat's backpack.
"Duck! Duck!" yelled Splat.

“Where? Where?” yelled Plank, looking blank.

Too late . . .

The duck with the little book

sat on Plank's head.

"No quack!" said Splat.

"No quack?" asked Spike

"No quack?" asked Plank.

"No quack!" said Splat.

“A duck lacking in quacking,”

said Spike and Plank.

“That’s not right.”

"Maybe Duck is hungry," said Spike.

Spike took the fish-stick snack

from Splat's backpack

and gave it to Duck.

But Duck didn't bite.
So Spike ate the fish-stick
snack himself.

"Maybe Duck is sad and needs to be cheered up," said Plank.

Plank made a funny face.

Duck didn't laugh.

Duck didn't even grin.

Plank's funny face stayed stuck.

"I know, I know!" said Kitten.
"Duck needs a bow
with a little pink dress to match.
That will bring Duck's quack back."

But the bow and the dress
were not a success.
Duck's beak stayed firmly closed.
"Mrs. Wimpydimple will know
what to do," said Splat.

Mrs. Wimpydimple looked at the duck.

"A duck lacking in quacking?"

she asked.

"How very odd.

But the answer must be simple,"

said Mrs. Wimpydimple.

"I will examine this duck
with the little book,"
said Mrs. Wimpydimple.
She played some music
to test Duck's ears.

Duck danced a merry duck dance.

"Duck's hearing is all right.

Maybe the problem

is Duck's eyesight,"

said Mrs. Wimpydimple.

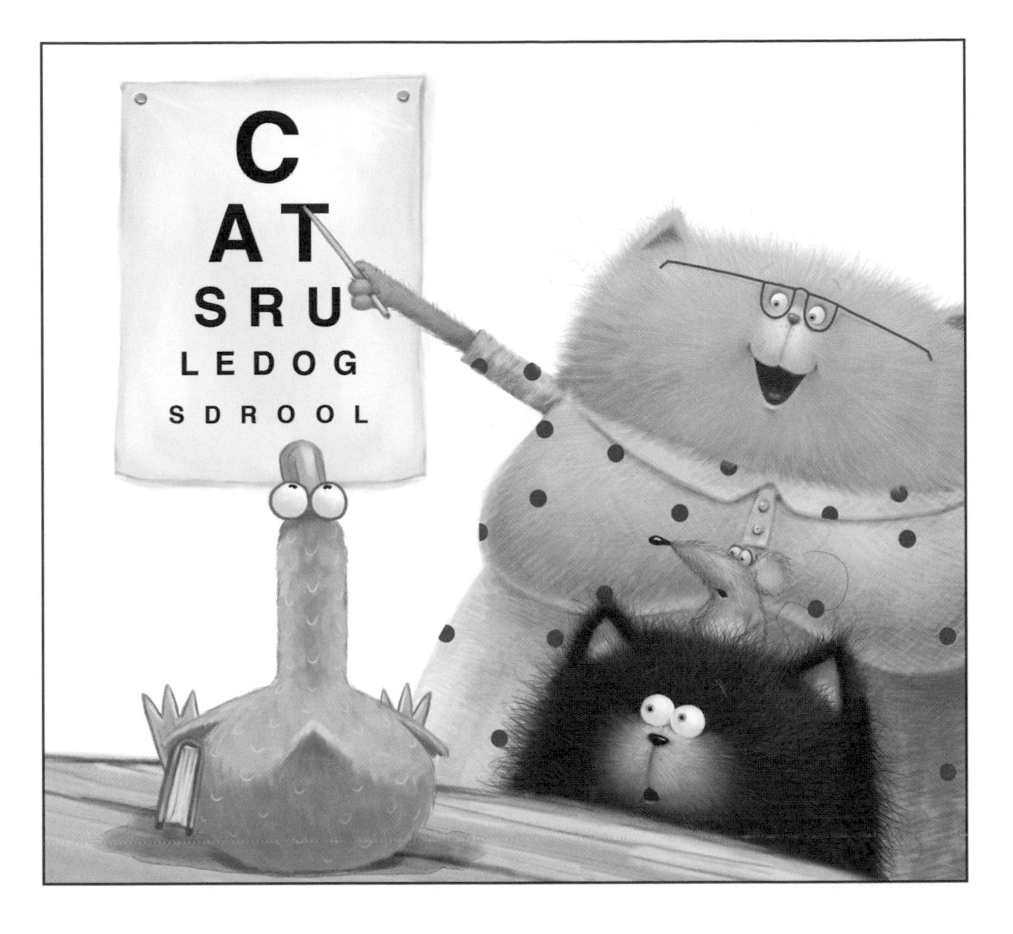

Mrs. Wimpydimple pointed to a chart.

Duck just looked blank.

She looked closely at Duck.

"Hmmm . . . I see," she said.

"But I don't think Duck does."

Mrs. Wimpydimple put her glasses
on Duck's beak.
Duck blinked.
Duck opened the book
and started to read out loud.

As he read, Duck began to quack.

"Quack . . . quack, quack . . ."

Followed by a "quack, quack, quack."

"Hooray for Duck!"

cheered the helpful cats.

Duck's quack was back.

And that was that.